Christmas Cocktails

AND SHENANIGANS

Christmas Cocktails
AND SHENANIGANS

GROWNUP CHRISTMAS STORIES
PAIRED WITH FESTIVE COCKTAILS
TO SHAKE UP YOUR HOLIDAYS

YELENA ANTER

Cocktail Vision

COCKTAIL VISION

Christmas Cocktails And Shenanigans: Grownup Christmas Stories Paired With Festive Cocktails To Shake Up Your Holidays by Yelena Anter
Published by Cocktail Vision Press
©CocktailVision2020
Recipe creation and testing: Yelena Anter
Cover and interior photography: Yelena Anter
Written by: Yelena Anter
Story editing: Gary Anter
Art direction, book design and styling: Cilicia Reavey
Cover design and photo editing: Cilicia Reavey
Copyright registration #: TXu 2-273-235
ISBN: 978-0-578-95957-3
First Edition. First Printing.

THE ACKNOWLEDGMENTS

This book would not exist without the encouragement and support of my loving husband Gary. You have always accepted my ups and downs and embraced all of my crazy ideas. Thank you for your patience, endless conversations, being my royal taster and my editor in chief. I love you forever!

Special thanks to Paul Edward and my beloved Chef Rubber family for empowering me with unlimited culinary resources, education, unconditional love and infinite faith in me. You have always inspired me to push my limits and believed I could do something great.

Thank you to my parents for all of the hard work, energy and sacrifice you have done to ensue I can pursue my most impossible dreams.

I raise my glass to all of my friends and Instagram cocktail community. Thank you for your friendship, inspiration and support. This book is for you!

To my brilliant editor and designer, Cilicia Reavey. Thank you for the passion and endless amount of care that it took to bring my Christmas Shenanigans to life!

The Contents

The Cocktails

Yelena

THE INTRO

Christmas casts a warm glow over people from all corners of the earth, each culture expressing Christmas joy in unique fashion. Here in The United States, we put the trendiest presents under a colorfully-decorated tree. But in my home town of Rybinsk, tangerines and walnuts are wrapped in shimmering gold foil and lovingly set onto the tree.

Where I'm from, decorations are the present — a precious fruit or nut impossible to find on the shelves of the typical Russian grocery store. The magic and joy of Christmas I felt as a young girl was no less poignant and meaningful than were I raised anywhere else on earth.

This book is an expression of my passion for the universal magic of Christmas, its unique ingredients, and the cocktails it has inspired me to create and share with you.

Salud, Santa! Cheers, Kris Kringle! And To Your Health, Father Frost!

1

Sugarplum's Mischiefs

"Are you sure you'll help me?" Sugarplum asks, smiling sheepishly and batting long sparkling eyelashes. Dainty fingers tangled together at the top of her tutu, she is a kaleidoscope vision of glimmering innocence with the promise of mischief.

Wood creaking, Nutcracker nods his head in admiration. "I am at your disposal, Sugarplum." Though it happens to be her name, he fancies calling her that as a nickname. Infatuated, there's probably nothing he wouldn't do for her. It's a romance most would judge impossible; but in a kingdom of joy and dreams, there's always room for hope.

A wicked twinkle lights up her periwinkle eyes, knowing she has him wrapped around her sweet little finger. Wings aflutter, she fills the air with sparkles that reflect in her eyes. "Whatever you do, don't get caught."

NAUGHTY SANGRIA

SERVES 6

THE INGREDIENTS
1 bottle your favorite chilled rosé
2 cups grapefruit rose vodka
½ cup amaro ramazzotti
¼ cup almond liqueur
1 honeycrisp apple, sliced
2 oranges, sliced
1 lemon, sliced
1 lime, sliced
1 pink grapefruit, sliced
½ oz vanilla extract
1 cup of sparkling pink grapefruit soda

THE GLASSWARE glass pitcher or glass drink dispenser

THE GARNISH a grapefruit wheel and sliced grapes

THE METHOD
In a large pitcher, combine first ten ingredients. Stir carefully and refrigerate for 2-6 hours.

Add pink grapefruit soda. Serve over ice.

SUGARPLUM'S MISCHIEFS

SERVES 1

THE INGREDIENTS
1½ oz gin
½ oz pimm's
1 oz plum wine
½ oz plum juice
½ oz fresh lime juice
2 oz tonic water

THE GLASSWARE a cocktail glass

THE RIM apply high viscosity simple syrup, or rim glue, onto the glass with a brush. sprinkle with pink sugar and set aside.

THE GARNISH a sugared plum

THE METHOD
Combine first five ingredients in a cocktail shaker with ice. Shake vigorously to chill and dilute.

Double-strain into a cocktail glass. Top it off with tonic water.

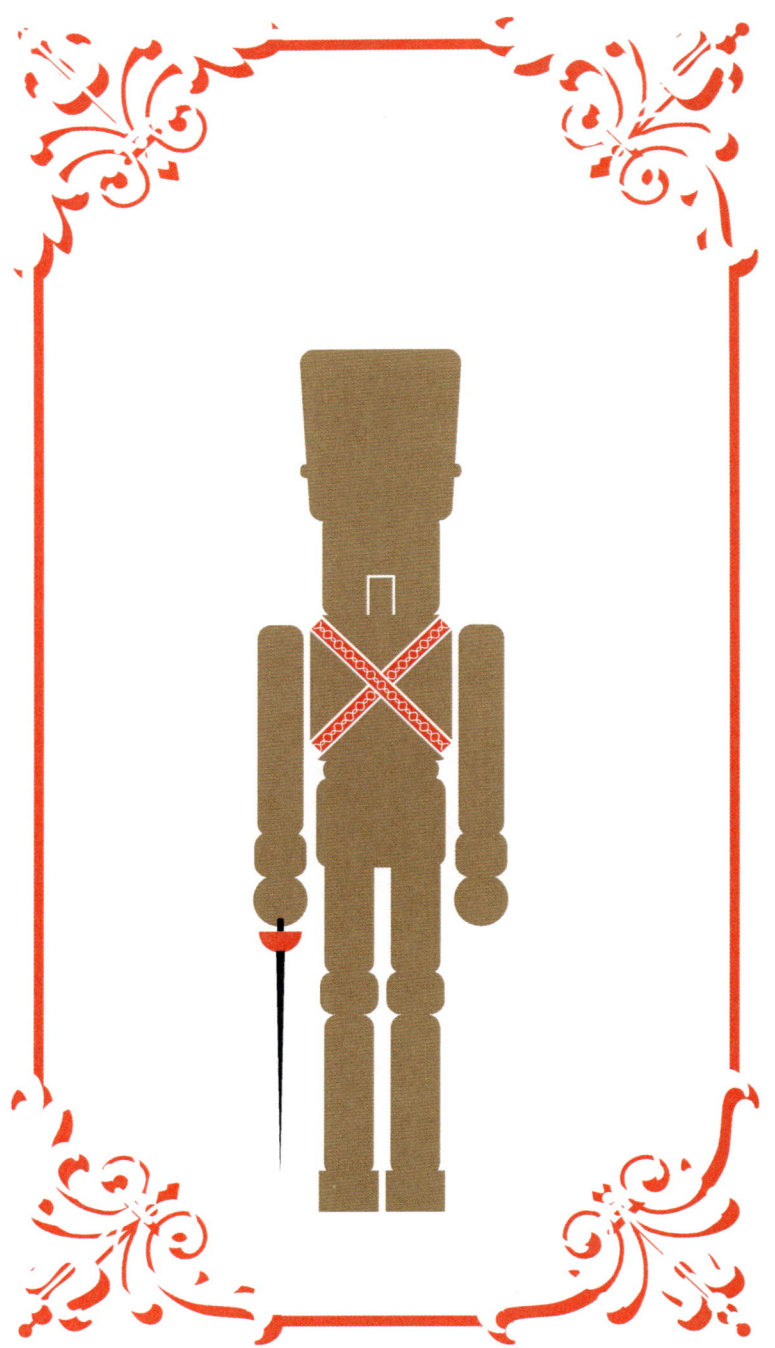

2

Nuts For The Nutcracker

Resting his hand solidly on the hilt of his wooden sword, Nutcracker responds, "I'm a soldier, Sugarplum. They'll never even know I was there." A trained professional, he's willing to take on any dangerous, yet noble, mission.

Nutcracker's attention is drawn by Sugarplum's deliciously sweet perfume, as she approaches close enough to whisper in his ear, "I believe in you." His heart skips a beat as he fantasizes of unwrapping such a beautiful present on Christmas morning. She gives him a peck on the cheek, sending his heart racing as she flies away.

NUTS FOR THE NUTCRACKER

SERVES 1

THE INGREDIENTS
1½ oz cognac
¾ oz hazelnut liqueur
½ oz fresh lemon juice
pinch of salt
3 oz brown ale
freshly grated nutmeg

THE GLASSWARE a chilled rocks glass

THE RIM attach nuts to the glass using melted chocolate. You can also use chopped or ground nuts, attaching them to the rim with high viscosity simple syrup or rim glue.

THE NUTS
brazil nut, chestnut, sacha inchi, pistachio, almond, marcona almond, cashew, macadamia, pecan, hazelnut, peanut, macambo

THE METHOD
Add the first four ingredients into a mixing glass with ice. Mix well. Add brown ale and stir gently to combine.

Pour into a chilled cocktail glass. Dust the top with some freshly grated nutmeg.

3

What Happens At The North Pole, Stays At The North Pole

A mere week before Christmas, all residents of the North Pole are preparing for their busiest night of the year. While Sugarplum and Nutcracker plot to release the Elves and distract Santa, Mrs. Claus has been making a move of her own. Not seeking to draw attention to her plan and upset her husband, she has recruited her unsuspecting mother to do her dirty work.

Mrs. Claus pulls a fruitcake from the oven, filling the kitchen air with a mouthwatering aroma as sumptuous and warm as the season. "Be a dear and take this to Mr. Grinch, won't you Mother? Tell him there's more where this came from."

WHAT HAPPENS AT THE NORTH POLE, STAYS AT THE NORTH POLE

SERVES 1

THE INGREDIENTS

2 oz gin
¼ oz blue curaçao orange liqueur
½ oz fresh lemon juice
½ oz fresh lime juice
¾ oz simple syrup
1 oz heavy cream or coconut milk
1 egg white
2 drops rose water
1 oz club soda

THE GLASSWARE a chilled highball glass

THE GARNISH juniper berries or fresh rosemary

THE METHOD

Add the first eight ingredients into a cocktail shaker. Dry-shake it (without ice) for 30-60 seconds.

Add five ice cubes and shake vigorously until all the ice dissolves (about one minute).

Double-strain into a chilled cocktail glass and top it off with club soda.

HOLIDAY VINO

SERVES 6

THE INGREDIENTS
1 bottle red wine
½ cup apple brandy
1 orange, sliced
6 whole cloves
3 cinnamon sticks, plus more for garnish
3 star anise
1 vanilla bean
¼ cup honey

THE GLASSWARE a heated restaurant glass.

THE GARNISH a citrus slice and a cinnamon stick

THE METHOD
In a medium saucepan, combine all ingredients. Bring to a simmer. Simmer on low for 10 minutes.

Serve hot in a heated restaurant glass.

4

Enchanted Mr. Grinch

As the forest path breaks into the familiar sight of the cabin, its front door opens in anticipation of her approach. Grinch steps forward through the doorway with a welcoming, yet crooked smile. Into the flirtatious, if not creepy green hands of Grinch, she places her daughter's basket of homemade goodies.

Unexpectedly, he pulls her into his embrace and kisses her gently. As dazed by his move as she is by the realization of her daughter's intentions, Grandma understands Grinch's powerful, if misplaced, emotion. All this while, she has forgotten to tell Grinch the care packages are from her daughter!

ENCHANTED MR. GRINCH

SERVES 1

THE INGREDIENTS
1½ oz gin
¼ oz absinthe
¼ oz green chartreuse
½ oz fresh lemon juice
1 oz pineapple juice
1 oz green juice
1½ oz ginger beer

THE GLASSWARE a tall highball glass

THE GARNISH fresh rosemary, mint or a floral element tied to the outside of the glass

THE METHOD
Combine all ingredients except for ginger beer in a cocktail shaker with ice. Shake vigorously to chill and dilute.

Double-strain into a tall cocktail glass with fresh ice. Top it off with ginger beer.

5

What Happened To Grandma?

Stammering away in shock, Grandma regains composure and returns to the outskirts of Santa's Village. Grinch's unsolicited and unexpected kiss stirs long-forgotten desires in her, as she begins daydreaming about the youthful and spirited masculinity of Santa's Elves.

Grandma is startled from her lustful fantasies with the shout, "watch out, Grannie! I can't steer this thing!" Excited to be let out early by Nutcracker and knowing Santa's preoccupation with auditions for this year's Christmas Tree Topper, the Elves have all climbed aboard Santa's new snowmobile for a quick joy ride over to the Candy Cane Club.

With seemingly no escape for Grandma, Santa's favorite deer Rudolf flies in out of nowhere. With lightning speed, he sweeps her off her feet and out of danger from the careening snowmobile. Standing over Grandma, bright red nose glowing with pride, Rudolf asks, "Are you okay?" Dazed and confused, Grandma mumbles, "Oh dear, you must be a snow angel." He laughs. "No, not me, Grannie. I'm Rudy!"

WHAT HAPPENED TO GRANDMA?

SERVES 1

THE INGREDIENTS
2 oz tequila blanco
2 oz fresh blood orange juice
½ oz fresh lime juice
3 oz ginger beer
fresh mint

THE GLASSWARE a tall cocktail glass

THE GARNISH fresh mint and candied ginger antlers. For ginger antlers, thinly slice fresh ginger on a cross-section. sprinkle with sugar and allow to sit overnight to crystallize.

THE METHOD
Add all ingredients to a tall cocktail glass. Fill with ice.

6

Santa's Den

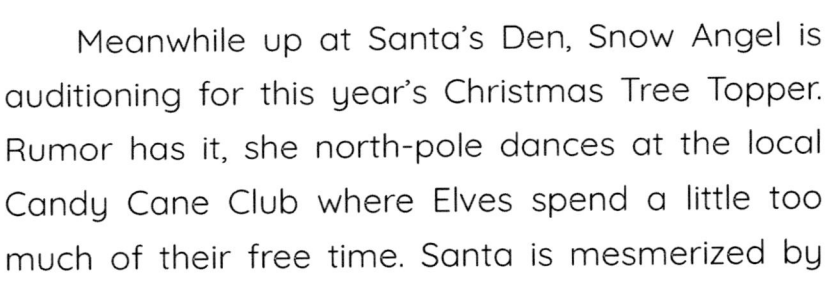

Meanwhile up at Santa's Den, Snow Angel is auditioning for this year's Christmas Tree Topper. Rumor has it, she north-pole dances at the local Candy Cane Club where Elves spend a little too much of their free time. Santa is mesmerized by her fluid, seductive pole moves, considering her a strong candidate to top this year's Christmas Tree.

Satisfied with the distraction caused by Nutcracker releasing the Elves, Sugarplum heads over to Santa's Den hoping for some romantic time alone with him. She imagines running her dainty fingers through his cotton candy beard, inhaling his sweet eggnog breath and snuggling into his velvety red coat, whispering into his ear what she desires most this Christmas and all the sugar treats she'd like to give him in return.

With all the strength she can muster, Sugarplum pulls on the massive wooden door of Santa's Den. The seasonal scent of holiday spice in the warm air is punctuated by something foreign, something cold, something threatening. She sees Santa reclined in fascination looking up at Snow Angel performing some provocative move, causing waves of jealousy to course through her.

SANTA'S OLD FASHIONED

SERVES 1

THE INGREDIENTS
2 oz bourbon
½ oz strawberry syrup
3 drops of vanilla extract
1 large muddled strawberry
2 dashes festive bitters

THE GLASSWARE a rocks glass

THE GARNISH a strawberry santa's hat and fresh mint. to create a strawberry santa's hat attach mini marshmallows to a strawberry using melted white chocolate.

THE METHOD
In a mixing glass muddle one large strawberry. Add bourbon, vanilla, strawberry syrup and ice. Mix thoroughly.

Double-strain into a cocktail glass over a large ice cube. Add bitters.

CHRISTMAS SPIRIT

SERVES 1

THE INGREDIENTS
2 oz bourbon
½ oz christmas cordial*
½ oz maple syrup
¾ oz fresh tangerine juice
¼ oz fresh lime juice
3 dashes festive bitters
splash *st. bernardus christmas ale*

THE GLASSWARE a chilled rocks glass

THE GARNISH a pine branch or fresh rosemary

THE METHOD
Combine the first five ingredients in a cocktail shaker with ice. Shake vigorously to chill and dilute.

Double-strain into a chilled cocktail glass over a large ice rock. Add a splash of ale and bitters.

*see recipe on following page

CHRISTMAS CORDIAL

SERVES 8

THE INGREDIENTS
1 cup water
½ cup sugar
zest of 1 lemon
3 oz of fresh lemon juice, (2 lemons)
4 oz of spruce or fir needles

THE METHOD
Bring everything to boil. Reduce the heat and simmer 2 hours.

Strain through a fine-mesh sieve. Repeat if needed to remove all the needles. Let cool completely.

7

Ginger On A Run

In that instant, Gingerbread Man sprints past Sugarplum, crumbs of cookie and frosting breaking off with every stride. In heavy pursuit, a white furry creature of immense size and strength barges into the room, barely fitting through the doorway. Sugarplum jumps into Santa's lap, saving her from being trampled by the massive intruder.

Immersed in the seductive movements of Snow Angel's audition, Santa awakes to the growing pandemonium around him. On his lap is a shaken Sugarplum, at his feet and surrounded in crumbs is the frightened Gingerbread Man, and towering at his threshold is the Abominable Snowman. "What is all of this damned commotion?"

Hyperventilating, Gingerbread Man musters what remains of his strength and cries out, "this monster was chasing me, Santa! I lost all of my buttons!"

"I thought we talked about this, Snowman! You promised years ago never to assault citizens of the North Pole ever again! What do you have to say for yourself?"

"Hungry for milkies and cookies, I am, Santa!" Snowman is a little confused. After all, this Gingerbread Man is just a cookie, and Snowman has eaten very little this winter.

"Gingerbread Man is not merely a cookie, he is one of my subjects under my protection! Because you have broken your vow not to harm people of this land, you shall spend time in service of The Grinch! But first, be a good lad and install Snow Angel atop my Christmas Tree. I've decided she is this year's tree topper."

MILKIES & COOKIES

SERVES 1

THE INGREDIENTS
2 oz spiced rum
½ oz jägermeister
3 oz eggnog
freshly grated nutmeg

THE GLASSWARE a chilled glass or milk bottle

THE GARNISH a rolled tuile straw and a gingerbread man cookie tied to the outside of the bottle

THE METHOD
Add all ingredients into a cocktail shaker with ice. Shake vigorously to chill and dilute.

Double-strain into a chilled glass or milk bottle. Finish it off with some freshly grated nutmeg.

ABOMINABLE BLUE BALL

SERVES 1

THE INGREDIENTS
2 oz butterfly pea flower infused gin
¼ oz maraschino liqueur
¼ oz crème de violette
¼ oz simple syrup
¼ oz fresh lemon juice

THE GLASSWARE a chilled martini glass or clean glass ornament bauble

THE GARNISH fresh rosemary

THE METHOD
Add all ingredients into a cocktail shaker with ice. Shake vigorously to chill and dilute.

Double-strain into a chilled cocktail glass.

GINGER ON A RUN

SERVES 1

THE INGREDIENTS
2 oz gingerbread infused irish whiskey*
½ oz clément créole shrubb
¼ oz goldschläger
1 oz fresh orange juice
½ oz fresh lemon juice
1 bar spoon pumpkin butter
pinch of cayenne pepper
2 oz ginger beer
salted cacao bitters

THE GLASSWARE chilled cocktail glass

THE RIM gingerbread cookie crumble applied to the glass using high viscosity simple syrup or rim glue

THE GARNISH gingerbread man cookie

THE METHOD
Add the first seven ingredients into a cocktail shaker with ice. Shake it up well.

Double-strain into a chilled cocktail glass. Top it off with ginger beer. Add a dash of bitters.

*see recipe on following page

GINGERBREAD INFUSED IRISH WHISKEY

SERVES 4

THE INGREDIENTS
1 cup of irish whiskey
2 gingerbread cookies

THE METHOD
In a mason jar, combine irish whiskey and gingerbread cookies. Seal tightly and let stand for six to eight hours, shaking it up occasionally.

Strain through a super fine mesh or a nut milk bag to get rid of all the solids. Best to use right away or keep refrigerated in a clean jar.

8

Snow Angel

With the long face of a scolded child, Snowman lumbers across the room to the Christmas Tree, a seismic lurching of white beastly fur. He sees Snow Angel in that instant, immediately entranced by her seductive beauty as his stride softens. Everyone in the quiet room sees his expression change to infatuation.

Knowing her effect upon men, the dancer climbs into the uncharacteristically gentle paw of the massive creature as they lock eyes. "Finally someone who can handle me," is a thought she considers for the very first time in her life.

SNOW ANGEL

SERVES 1

THE INGREDIENTS
2 oz coconut cream liqueur
1 oz vanilla vodka
1 oz crème de cacao blanc liqueur

THE GLASSWARE chilled margarita glass

THE RIM sprinkles to the outside of the glass by using high viscosity simple syrup or rim glue

THE GARNISH soy paper angel wings

THE METHOD
Blend all ingredients in a blender with a quarter cup of ice.

9

Oh, Santa!

"Well with that matter resolved..." Santa gazes down with benevolence at the fairy in his lap. "Sugarplum, do you have a special wish I can fulfill?" All of her jealousy washed away, Sugarplum draws in close to the red velvet of Santa's coat, looks up at him, and bats her eyelashes flirtatiously. "Oh Santa! I thought you'd never ask!" She yearns to whisper naughty desires into his ear.

10

Who Let The Elves Out?

Marching in with such incredible haste that his wooden joints are heard far away, Nutcracker rushes into the Den. "Mr. Claus, we have a problem!" Scanning the quiet room of faces staring back at him, Nutcracker's eyes meet Sugarplum's. Stunned by the sight of his beloved in Santa's lap, Nutcracker's heart drops as everything tunes out.

"How may I help you, Soldier?" Santa asks. Unable to respond for several moments, Nutcracker is brought back to the emergency at hand. "Sir, the Elves crashed your snowmobile into the toy factory's power supply. Our entire manufacturing process has come to a halt!"

"Why were the Elves not at the workshop under your supervision? How did they gain access to my snowmobile? This is unimaginably horrible news! It's likely we may be forced to cancel Christmas if power is not restored!" Santa's demeanor changes from judicious to what can only be described as desperate.

Feeling guilty for succumbing to Sugarplum's deception, Nutcracker clears his throat in preparation for telling Santa the whole truth. "Sir, I let the Elves out -" Suddenly, Nutcracker is interrupted by the newest arrival into the room.

WHO LET THE ELVES OUT?

SERVES 1

THE INGREDIENTS
1½ oz gin
¾ oz sour apple liqueur
¾ oz fresh lime juice
¼ oz green chartreuse
1½ oz ginger beer

THE GLASSWARE a chilled martini glass

THE METHOD
Add first four ingredients into a cocktail shaker with ice. Shake vigorously to chill and dilute.

Double-strain into chilled glass. Top it off with ginger beer.

11

Mrs. Boss

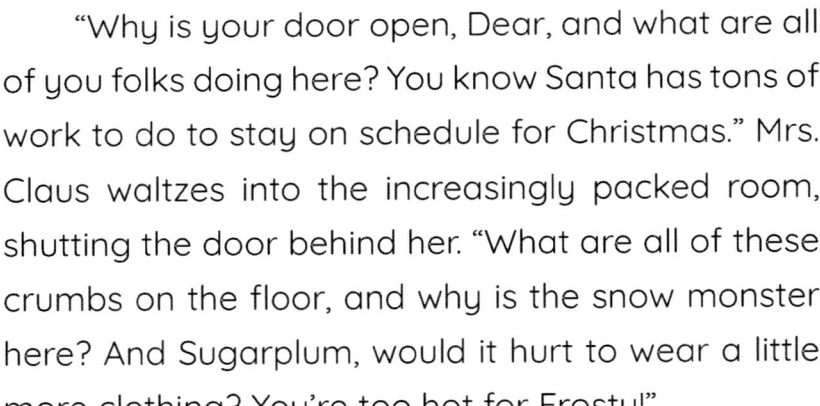

"Why is your door open, Dear, and what are all of you folks doing here? You know Santa has tons of work to do to stay on schedule for Christmas." Mrs. Claus waltzes into the increasingly packed room, shutting the door behind her. "What are all of these crumbs on the floor, and why is the snow monster here? And Sugarplum, would it hurt to wear a little more clothing? You're too hot for Frosty!"

"Darling, we've had a very busy day, as you can see. I'll catch you up over dinner tonight. In the meantime, we have a real problem on our hands. According to Nutcracker here, the Elves have destroyed the power supply to our toy factory! I'm afraid Christmas won't proceed as planned!"

HOTS FOR FROSTY

SERVES 1

THE INGREDIENTS
2 oz chocolate whiskey
½ oz peppermint liqueur
1 oz hot espresso
2 oz hot cocoa
pinch of salt
pinch of cayenne

THE GLASSWARE a glass mug

THE GARNISH mini marshmallows and fresh mint

THE METHOD
Combine all the ingredients. Serve in your favorite
Christmas mug. Heat it up in the microwave or
serve over ice.

12

Fruitcake Confusion

A loud knocking sound focuses everyone's attention at the door. Who else could this be, they all wonder? "Come on in!" Santa bellows with strained authority. The door creaks open as everyone stares in disbelief of the sight of Grinch. Not only does he never visit Christmas Village, he's decked out in his finest purple holiday suit. Grinch saunters in, a massive sack on his back and asks, "Where's Grandma?"

Momentarily elated by the sight of Grinch and the notion he came all this way to see her, Mrs. Claus comes to the quick realization her Mother never returned from the errand she put her on earlier that day. She responds with concern and hesitation, "I'll search for her; in the meantime, please take a load off and make yourself comfortable Mr. Grinch."

"Thank you, but I'd rather not. I have a present for Grandma. Her fruitcakes are delicious," he responds with a wide grin.

"Her fruitcakes?" It occurs to Mrs. Claus she was not identified as the actual gift-giver. Her genuine concern for her mother's safety overrides any sense of petty grievance, as she makes a turn for the door.

SUCH A FRUITCAKE

SERVES 1

THE INGREDIENTS
1½ oz rum
1 oz scotch
½ oz amaretto
¼ oz frangelico
¼ oz jägermeister
¼ oz orange liqueur
¼ oz sweet vermouth
1 oz fresh lemon juice
1 oz fresh orange juice
3 dashes of aromatic bitters
cinnamon sprinkle

THE GLASSWARE a highball glass or mason jar

THE GARNISH various fruit wheels

THE METHOD
Add first nine ingredients into a cocktail shaker with ice. Shake vigorously to chill and dilute.

Double-strain into cocktail glass, over fresh ice. Add bitters and cinnamon.

13

Chillin' With My Snowmies

"You two fellows gave me such a holly, jolly time tonight!" Grandma exclaims loudly as she stammers in, escorted by an elf on each arm.

"What do we have here, Mother?" Mrs. Claus asks, hands on her hips in disbelief and disapproval. "I was just about to search the North Pole for you!"

"These handsome gentlemen and I had drinks at the Candy Cane Club. What a marvelous place, with lovely angels dancing everywhere! And the hot toddies were phenomenal!"

"You were where? The Candy Cane Club is not where you find respectable gentlemen, Mother. It's where you find mischievous elves! I can't leave you alone for a moment!" Mrs. Claus reprimands.

"I'm not a child, Dearie, and I won't be deprived of a little happiness from a woman who can't deliver her fruitcakes to the man she has a crush on," Grandma defends herself.

"How dare you, Mother, you're lit as a Christmas Tree!" Mrs. Claus fires back.

"Just because I know how to have fun doesn't mean I'm inebriated. I was just chillin' with my snowmies and got a little tipsy!" Grandma replies.

CHILLIN' WITH MY SNOWMIES

SERVES 1

THE INGREDIENTS
2 oz moonshine
½ oz vanilla liqueur
½ oz goldschläger
1½ oz piña colada mix
festive bitters
freshly grated nutmeg

THE GLASSWARE chilled cocktail glass

THE RIM marshmallow dust. to make, grind a dried marshmallow in a coffee grinder.

THE GARNISH a marshmallow snowman

THE METHOD
Add first four ingredients into a cocktail shaker with ice. Shake well.

Double-strain into a chilled cocktail glass. Add a dash of bitters. Sprinkle with fresh nutmeg.

HOTTY TODDY

SERVES 1

THE INGREDIENTS
1½ oz cognac
½ oz honey liqueur
½ oz fresh lemon juice
1 tsp honey
your favorite festive holiday tea

THE GLASSWARE a glass mug

THE GARNISH a lemon slice, whole vanilla bean
and a honey comb

THE METHOD
Steep your favorite holiday tea according to the
directions in three quarters of a cup of hot water.

Add honey and let it dissolve completely.

Add cognac, honey liqueur and lemon juice.

14

Blame It On The Mistletoe

Having heard quite enough of the two women in his life, but nothing from his elves, Santa asks, "And what do you have to say for yourselves? Your actions today have not only distressed my wife and confused my mother-in-law, but they've put Christmas in jeopardy!"

Grinch interrupts, "You people are ridiculous, every single one of you." Looking directly now at Grandma, he adds, "I thought your fruitcakes were genuine. I hiked all the way up here to give you a Christmas gift," and staring directly at Mrs. Claus, "only to find each of you deceiving each other. It's confusing and rather tiresome." Wanting none of their antics, Grinch strides out, dropping his gift sack on the floor behind him.

BLAME IT ON THE MISTLETOE

SERVES 1

THE INGREDIENTS
1 oz gin
1 oz pomegranate liqueur
½ oz pomegranate juice
3 oz champagne

THE GLASSWARE a chilled champagne flute

THE RIM festive sprinkles with high viscosity simple syrup or rim glue

THE METHOD
Add first three ingredients in a cocktail shaker with ice. Shake to chill and dilute.

Double-strain into a chilled flute. Carefully top it off with champagne.

15

The Gift

With an incredibly loud thud, the sack busts open and releases its dark, dusty contents onto the floor. As the cloud of dust settles, what appears is the shining glimmer of pure, black coal in all shapes and sizes.

"That's the oddest gift I've ever received," Grandma breaks the silence, and looking at her daughter, "but you should have it, Dearie. It suits you."

SOMEONE'S BEEN NAUGHTY...

SERVES 1

THE INGREDIENTS
1½ oz spiced rum
½ oz jägermeister
½ oz pomegranate liqueur
¼ oz absinthe
1 oz pomegranate juice
¼ oz fresh lemon juice
splash of cola or root beer

THE GLASSWARE a rocks glass or carved out pomegranate that looks like santa's sack

THE GARNISH black licorice pieces

THE METHOD
Add the first six ingredients into a cocktail shaker with ice. Shake vigorously to chill and dilute.

Double-strain into the drink vessel of your choice. Top it off with cola or root beer.

16

A Partridge In A Pear Tree

Quiet all this while, it suddenly occurs to Nutcracker a means of saving Christmas! Speaking directly to Santa he implores, "Sir, I believe we've found a solution to our energy problem at the toy factory."

"By George, you're brilliant, Nutcracker! We'll use this coal to fuel the manufacturing lines!" Directly to the elves, Santa adds, "You two will follow Nutcracker's every instruction to get the toy factory up and running. Make haste, as we have no time to lose if we are to stay on schedule!" With that, Nutcracker and the Elves start gathering up the coal, relieved to have escaped Santa's wrath, and optimistic of the work that lay ahead.

"I believe Grinch may have saved Christmas, Darling," Mrs. Claus warmly suggests to Santa. "He's no Partridge in a Pear Tree, but he's certainly given us hope this Christmas," Santa responds with a wink. He caringly sets Sugarplum down, and rises from his chair with instructions for everyone:

"Snowman, stop flirting with Snow Angel, and put her atop my tree where she belongs. When you're don't with that, go help my elves. They could certainly use a little muscle. Under no circumstances are you to eat anyone!"

"And Grandma, could you frost Gingerbread Man a new set of clothes?"

A PARTRIDGE IN A PEAR TREE

SERVES 1

THE INGREDIENTS
2 oz pear brandy
1 oz pear liqueur
¼ oz cinnamon liqueur
¼ oz honey simple syrup

THE GLASSWARE a chilled cocktail glass

THE GARNISH fresh or candied pear

THE METHOD
Combine all ingredients in a cocktail mixing glass with ice. Stir to chill and dilute.

Double-strain into a chilled cocktail glass.

17

Timeless Love

"As for you, my Dear, I believe I owe you a romantic sleigh ride dinner tonight. Let's leave these shenanigans and make some mischief of our own."

Later that evening, Mrs. Claus regards her husband with admiration as he deftly steers the sleigh past the outskirts of town. Under the magical glow of northern lights, she basks in the joy of her timeless love for the greatest man she has ever known in all of the North Pole.

NORTHERN LIGHTS

SERVES 1

THE INGREDIENTS
2 oz pisco
½ oz sour apple liqueur
1 oz fresh lime juice
½ oz simple syrup
1 egg white

THE GLASSWARE a chilled, stemmed glass

THE METHOD
Combine all ingredients in a cocktail shaker. Dry shake until frothy.

Add ice and shake vigorously for about a minute.

Double-strain into a chilled glass.

Carefully drizzle ¼ oz blue curaçao and 3 drops butterfly pea syrup to create a northern lights swirl.

CHRISTMAS SHENANIGANS

SERVES 1

THE INGREDIENTS
1½ oz candy cane infused vodka*
1½ oz vanilla vodka
¾ oz fresh lemon juice
1 oz tonic water

THE GLASSWARE a chilled martini glass

THE RIM crushed candy canes attached using high viscosity simple syrup or rim glue

THE GARNISH two candy canes in the shape of a heart

THE METHOD
Combine candy cane vodka, vanilla vodka and fresh lemon juice in a cocktail shaker with ice. Shake vigorously to chill and dilute.

Double-strain into a chilled martini glass. Top it off with tonic water.

*see recipe on following page

CANDY CANE VODKA

SERVES 4-5

THE INGREDIENTS

2 standard candy canes
1 cup vodka, unflavored

THE METHOD

Allow candy canes to fully dissolve in vodka.

Christmas Shenanigans

THE GLOSSARY

THE SPIRITS & BOOZ

ABSINTHE

Absinthe is an anise-flavored spirit made by steeping wormwood and other aromatic herbs such as hyssop, lemon balm, and angelica in alcohol. Banned in the United States in 1912 due to its alleged dangerous properties, it was made legal again in 2007.

One of my favorites is St. George Absinthe Verte.

AMARETTO

Amaretto is a sweet Italian liquor flavored from bitter almonds, apricot stones and peach stones.

Disaronno is my go-to.

AMARO

Amaro is a bitter Italian liqueur made with a blend of roots, herbs, and orange peel.

Amaro Ramazzoti is my favorite brand.

BOURBON

Bourbon is a type of American whiskey, a barrel-aged distilled spirit primarily from corn. Although bourbon may be made anywhere in the United States, it predominates from Kentucky.

A few brands I love in cocktails are Angel's Envy, Whistle Pig, Four Roses, Blanton's and Woodford Reserve.

BRANDY

Brandy is the distillate of fermented grapes; though apple, apricot, peach, and other fruits can also be used to make brandy. Brandy is produced around the world as Cognac, Armagnac, pisco, and eau-de-vie among regional styles.

Some of my favorite brandies are Sullivan's Cove, St-Rémy and Paul Masson.

BROWN ALE

Brown ale is a style of English beer adopted by craft brewers in the United States and Scandinavia. Known for its mild bitterness, hoppy flavor and comforting malt flavors, this beer often has delicious notes of bread, caramel, chocolate, nuts, and raisins.

Nut Brown Ale by Samuel Smith Brewery, New Castle Brown Ale, Rogue Hazelnut, and New Belgian Dark Ale are great brown ales.

BUTTERFLY PEA FLOWER INFUSED GIN

Butterfly Pea Flower comprises an herbal tea of vibrant blue color and delicate floral flavor. Contact with anything acidic changes color to purple.

Empress 1908 is my favorite Butterfly Pea Flower Infused Gin; but if you can't find it at your local liquor store, simply add Butterfly Pea Flower powder or tea to your favorite gin or vodka until infused to your liking.

CANDY CANE INFUSED VODKA

Various brands come out with their own version of Candy Cane Vodka during the holidays; but if you can't find it at your local liquor store, simply add candy canes to your favorite unflavored vodka until dissolved.

CHAMPAGNE

Only sparkling wine from the Champagne region of France can be called Champagne. Non-vintage "brut" champagnes are typically the entry-level "house style" versions of most producers.

CHOCOLATE WHISKEY

Chocolate Whiskey is Whiskey infused with the decadent flavor of chocolate.

Whiskey Smith Co, 8 Ball Chocolate Whiskey and Bird Dog Whiskey are a few favorites.

CINNAMON LIQUEUR

Cinnamon liquors provide a welcomed sweet-and-spicy flavor profile that can be elegantly mixed into drinks.

A couple of brands to play with are Jack Daniel's Tennessee Fire Cinnamon Whiskey and Bird Dog Hot Cinnamon Whiskey.

COCONUT CREAM LIQUEUR

The low-alcohol nature of cream liqueurs make them approachable and easy to drink, enjoyed neat, on the rocks or added to your coffee or hot cocoa.

CocoSky Coconut Cream Liqueur and Hard Truth Toasted Coconut Rum Cream are a couple of favorite coconut versions.

COGNAC

Using Ugni blanc, Folle Blanche, and Colombard grape varietals, Cognac is a twice-distilled brandy made only in the Cognac region of France. Younger cognacs are perfect as the base of several classic cocktails, such as the Sidecar and Mint Julep.

Some of my favorite brands of Cognac are Courvoisier, Remy Martin, Martell and Hennessy.

CRÈME DE CACAO BLANC LIQUEUR

This white chocolate liqueur tastes of fresh ground roasted cocoa beans and has a savory nose. It is completely clear and will not change the appearance of your cocktail.

Some favorite brands are Drillaud, Giffard and Marie Brizard.

CRÈME DE VIOLETTE

This low-proof, dark blue liqueur made from the violet flower has a distinctly floral and sweet flavor profile. Crème de Violette is mixed with dry vermouth, served alone as a cordial, mixed with sparkling wines, or used in classic cocktails such as Aviation and Blue Moon.

Some well-regarded brands are The Bitter Truth, Benoit Serres and Rothman & Winter.

FRANGELICO

Frangelico is an Italian liqueur, comprised of a distilled spirit infused with macerated hazelnuts, cocoa, vanilla and other natural flavors. Enjoy Frangelico over ice, in a cocktail or added to coffee.

Other nut-flavored liqueurs include Bartenura, DeKuyper, Francesca, Hiram Walker, and Kahlua.

GIN

Originally a medicinal liquor made by monks and alchemists across Europe, gin is a distilled spirit flavored predominately with juniper berries and herbs.

Some of my favorite refined brands are Highclere Castle, Malfy, and The Botanist.

GRAPEFRUIT ROSE VODKA

Flavored Vodkas are some of the most versatile spirits around, easily mixed into a cocktail. Flavored vodkas are produced in a variety of fruit and spice flavors such as grapefruit, raspberry, vanilla, currant, chili pepper, apple, chocolate and banana, to name a few.

Ketel One Botanical Grapefruit Rose Vodka is one of my favorites, but can be substituted with any high-quality citrus-flavored vodkas.

GREEN CHARTREUSE

Green Chartreuse is a world-famous French liqueur with a uniquely natural green color and a secret recipe of 130 botanical plants passed down among the Carthusian monks of the French Alps.

The closest match to Green Chartreuse is Dolin Génépy from Haus Alpenz.

HONEY LIQUEUR

A wide variety of liqueurs are flavored with the sweet floral goodness of honey, easily sipped on the rocks, used to make hot toddies, and made to build cocktails.

Popular examples include Germany's Barenjager and the famous Polish Krupnik. You can also make your own honey liqueur by adding equal parts water and honey to your favorite whiskey, vodka, brandy or tequila.

JÄGERMEISTER

Unfortunately associated with wild parties, Jägermeister is a German herbal liqueur whose 80-year-old secret recipe includes 56 exotic botanicals such as green cardamom, Chinese star anise, Indian ginger root, and Ceylon cinnamon. Enjoy Jägermeister over ice or to elevate your cocktails to the next level.

LUXARDO MARASCHINO LIQUEUR

Luxardo Maraschino Liqueur is distilled from Luxardo sour marasca cherries, creating a smooth liqueur with persistent aromas of cherry and rosewater.

Alternatives include Natasha, Lazzarroni, Cherry Heering, and Kirsch.

MINT LIQUEUR

Whether blended in cold eggnog or added to a mug of hot chocolate, mint liqueur is synonymous with the winter holidays.

The most famous mint liqueur is crème de menthe, vodka flavored with dried Corsican mint or peppermint, and available in both green and white varieties.

DeKuyper, Gabriel Boudier, and Wondermint are go-to brands of mint liqueur.

ORANGE LIQUEUR

Orange liqueurs are a diverse group of distilled spirits flavored with a variety of orange citrus. Most are sweet and some use a neutral grain base while others feature a liquor such as brandy.

Orange liqueurs are produced in The Caribbean and Europe, named by their principal citrus fruit — triple sec, curaçao, Cointreau, and Grand Marnier.

PEAR LIQUEUR

An ideal ingredient in cocktails with brown spirits such as bourbon and brandy, pear liqueur features the fresh, earthy flavor of ripe pears. Add a splash of pear liqueur to sparkling wine or pair pear eau de vie with a rich cheese plate for dessert.

Favorite brands include St. George and Clear Creek Distillery. You can make pear liqueur yourself by infusing ripe pears in a dissolved solution of sugar water and brandy or vodka, and spicing it with cinnamon and vanilla.

PIMM'S LIQUEUR

Great Britain's Pimm's No. 1 Liqueur is a rich amber-hued infusion of gin, herbal botanicals, caramelized orange and delicate spices. Mix Pimm's with lemonade, mint, orange and strawberry slices and pour over ice for a refreshing cocktail called Pimm's Original.

PLUM WINE

Traditionally made from Japanese Ume plums fermented in sugar and yeast, plum wine features a rich, tart, aromatic and sweet flavor suitable as an aperitif. Beloved for their pinkish blossom during late winter and early spring, Ume plums thrive in China and Japan.

Choya, Takara, and Fu-ki are excellent plum wines.

POMEGRANATE LIQUEUR

Made with pomegranate juice, vodka and tequila, Pama by Heaven Hill Brands in Kentucky is the most popular brand of pomegranate-flavored liqueur.

Pama is ideal when added to a cocktail, sparkling wine or club soda.

RED WINE

Fermented from dark grape varietals, red wine can range in color from violet to brown, depending upon the barrel age of the wine. Red wine is ideal as a base for more complex cocktails. Mulled wine, also known as spiced wine, is a type of warm cocktail made with red wine and various mulling spices, served during the holidays.

ROSÉ

Featuring less color than red wine due to reduced contact of the grape flesh with the darker grape skins, rosé runs from sweet to dry. When mixing rosé into cocktails such as sangria, try a dry rosé of pinot noir instead of sweet rosés of riesling or moscato.

RUM

Rum is the distillate of fermented sugarcane molasses or sugarcane juice aged in oak barrels. Most rums are produced in The Caribbean, The Americas and other sugar-producing countries, such as The Philippines and India. Light rum, also known as white or silver rum, has virtually no color and a lighter flavor than its barrel-aged version.

Sailor Jerry, Captain Morgan, and Bacardi are some well known brands with a wide variety of choices from light, spiced, to flavored.

SPICED RUM

Aged for the same length of time as black rum, spiced rum adds spices and caramel coloring for a signature taste of sweet spice. Spiced rum is an extremely versatile spirit, enjoyed on its own or mixed into a wide variety of cocktails, both hot and cold.

SCOTCH

One of the most complex and nuanced spirits is Scotch whisky, a blend of malt whisky and/or grain whisky made in Scotland in a manner specified by law. The five Scotch Whisky regions are Campbeltown, Highland, Islay (pronounced 'eye-luh'), Lowland and Speyside, each offering a unique and time-honored expression of Scotch.

Campbeltown whisky is robust and rich in character, featuring hints of salt, smoke, leather, fruit, vanilla and toffee.
A couple of noteworthy Campbeltown whiskies are Springbank and Glen Scotia Victoriana.

Highland whisky ranges in character from light to salty coastal malts, options available for all palates.
McClelland's and Dalmore are excellent Highland Single Malts.

Islay is a magical island where the majority of its population are employed in the production of whisky.
Bunnahabhain and Bruichladdich epitomize the smoky, heavily-peated whiskies of Islay.

Lowland whisky is elegant and smooth with a fresh palate of honeysuckle, cream, ginger, toffee, toast and cinnamon.
Auchentoshan and Glenkinchie are good examples of Lowland malt whisky.

Speyside whisky, commonly matured in old Sherry casks, is characterized as lighter and featuring flavors of pear, honey, vanilla and spice.
Glenlivet, Glen Moray, and Balvenie are labels that embody Speyside whisky.

SOUR APPLE LIQUEUR

Sour Apple Liqueur, also known as Apple Pucker and Apple Schnapps, is a vibrant green, sweet and sour liqueur whose flavor profile mirrors that of Granny Smith green apples.

SWEET VERMOUTH

Vermouth is a fortified wine, aromatized and flavored with botanicals. Other than mixing in cocktails, vermouth is pleasant as an aperitif on the rocks with a lemon twist and perhaps a splash of soda or sparkling wine for a boozy spritz.

Dubonnet Rouge was created by Joseph Dubonnet in 1846 as a means of making medicinal quinine more palatable for the French Foreign Legion troops.

Mancino Rossi Amaranto is an ultra-complex vermouth made with 38 different botanicals, including juniper, vanilla, orange and rhubarb.

TEQUILA

Tequila is a distilled spirit made from agave azul (blue agave), from Jalisco, Guanajuato, Michoacan, Tamaulipas and Nayarit regions of Mexico. The types of tequila are blanco, joven, reposado, añejo and extra añejo.

Tequila Blanco (silver tequila) is the unaged expression of tequila, ideal for mixing a margarita.

Tequila joven contains a small amount of aged tequila blended into the unaged tequila.

Tequila reposado is aged in oak casks for at least two months and up to one year, whereas tequila añejo is aged for at least one year.

Añejo tequilas are enjoyed neat or employed as the base spirit in recipes calling for a dark spirit.

Extra añejo is a rare expression of tequila, aged for at least three years in oak casks.

Like tequila, mezcal is made from agave, but produced in Oaxaca, Mexico, where distillation is preceded by roasting the agave piña in an underground pit for a distinctly smoky flavor.

BREWED TEA

So many fun and festive tea varieties are available during the holidays. Visit the tea section of your local supermarket and follow the steeping instructions on the tea packaging. Steep black tea for 4-5 minutes, green and oolong teas for 3 minutes, and white tea for 4 minutes.

CITRUS JUICE

Freshly-squeezed citrus juice imparts great taste and myriad health benefits to tasty cocktails. To make your own, cut a lime, lemon or orange in half, and squeeze its fluid contents into a glass using your hands or a citrus reamer or citrus squeezer.

EGGNOG

Synonymous with Christmas, eggnog is made with milk, eggs, cream and sugar. Eggnog is typically served chilled mixed with brandy and garnished with ground nutmeg.

EGG WHITES

Imparting a rich body and silky texture to a cocktail, egg whites function to soften and balance powerful flavors. Acting as a canvas for heavier garnishes, a topping of egg white foam allows flower petals, citrus zest, or a dusting of chocolate to float on top.

To obtain the best egg white foam, shake all ingredients in a cocktail shaker without ice for a minute, then add ice and shake again for another minute. This double-shake method allows the egg whites time to develop their signature velvety texture.

ESPRESSO

Espresso is a coffee-making method of Italian origin, in which a small amount of nearly boiling water is forced under pressure through heavily-roasted, finely-ground coffee beans.

GINGER BEER

Made by fermenting a mixture of water, sugar, and ginger, ginger beer is a bubbly soft drink with a tangy, spicy flavor. It has a stronger flavor, less sweetness and fewer bubbles than ginger ale. Paired beautifully with any liquor, ginger beer is used to make a variety of cocktails from the Moscow mule to the Dark and Stormy.

My favorite ginger beers are Fever Tree and Regatta Mixers.

GREEN JUICE

Green juice contains several servings of fruit, vegetables, and other superfoods into a nutrient-dense beverage ideal for mixing into cocktails. If you can't find it bottled or freshly made at your local grocer, bring the following chopped ingredients into a blender for thirty seconds and then strain: cucumber, celery, apple, water, lemon, pineapple, mint and ginger.

Some quality brands of green juice are Suja, Bolthouse Farms, and Naked Juice.

HONEY

A superfood with tremendous benefits to the body and mind, honey has been used as medicine and food for hundreds of years. Over 300 uniquely-flavored varieties of honey exist, lightly-colored and delicately-flavored clover honey being the most common in the United States.

HOT COCOA

Hot cocoa, hot chocolate or drinking chocolate is a warm drink comprised of cocoa powder, heated milk, vanilla extract, and sugar whisked together and topped with whipped cream or marshmallows.

MAPLE SYRUP

Maple syrup is a natural and nutritious sweetener. It is usually made from the xylem sap of sugar maple, red or black maple trees. There are a lot of different brands on the market.

One of my favorite ones is by Runamok Maple from Cambridge, Vermont, with elegant packaging, innovative flavor profiles, and the highest quality ingredients.

PIÑA COLADA MIX

Piña Colada Mix is basically cream of coconut and pineapple juice with some lime. There are so many terrifically delicious cocktail mixers on the market.

Some of the most popular ones include Citra Fresh Agave Mixers, Chi-Chi's. It is very easy to make it yourself: Combine 1 cup cream of coconut, 3/4 cup pineapple juice and 3 tablespoons lime juice. Blend on medium speed until creamy. Keep refrigerated for up to a week.

PINEAPPLE JUICE

Pineapple juice comes in two versions, fresh and from concentrate. I always seek out the best ingredients for mixing in cocktails, so I recommend fresh pineapple juice.

Trader Joe's and Dole are excellent choices of pineapple juice.

PLUM JUICE

Packed with nutrients and antioxidants, plum juice contributes to good health and tasty cocktails when mixed with whiskey, brandy and other spirits.

POMEGRANATE JUICE

Rich in antioxidants, vitamins and other nutrients, pomegranate juice contributes to overall good health and great cocktails!

Fresh pomegranate juice brands include Lakewood PURE, FruitFast, and POM, while carbonated versions include San Pellegrino Pomegranate and Sprouts Organic Pomegranate Italian Soda.

SIMPLE SYRUP

This staple cocktail sweetener more than earns its name, consisting simply of equal-parts granulated sugar and water. You can infuse simple syrup with countless ingredients—including spices, herbs and fruit.

To make your own simple syrup, combine equal parts boiling water and granulated sugar until dissolved, then refrigerate. To make strawberry syrup, add equal parts strawberry slices, sugar and water, bring to a boil and simmer for 20 minutes, then strain the resulting mixture.

SPARKLING SODAS

The carbonated bubbles of sparkling soda elevate a cocktail to the next level by physically stimulating the tongue, creating refreshing acidity, and lifting aromatic molecules to the nose.

Carbonated soda juices come in endless flavor variations by companies such as Fever Tree, Spindrift, and Pellegrino.

THE GARNISH & SPICES

APPLES
Red Delicious, Gala, Granny Smith, Pink Lady, Golden Delicious, Honeycrisp, McIntosh are some other popular varieties of apple used to impart crisp acidity and sweet fruitiness to your cocktails.

BITTERS
Aromatic bitters are alcohol-based infusions of bittering botanicals such as gentian root, cinchona bark, and cassia with flavoring agents like fruit peels, spices, dried flowers, and herbs. Bitters are sold in small bottles and administered in drops to enhance the complexity of your cocktail.

Scrappy's, Bitternens and Peychaud's are common brands.

CINNAMON
Cinnamon is a spice made from strips of the inner bark of cinnamon trees that curl into rolls when dried. Cinnamon sticks are used as a festive garnish, while its ground powder is sprinkled on the surface of a cocktail or adhered to the rim of a cocktail glass.

CLOVES
The dried, unopened bud of the tropical evergreen clove tree can be used whole to infuse syrup liqueurs. Its ground version is used as a garnish on the surface of drinks for a pleasant, earthy floral flavor.

FRESH MINT
Used as a garnish, fresh mint elevates the color and aroma of the finest cocktails, adding a pop of color and a delicate aroma. To turn tired, packaged mint into fresher mint, revive the leaves in a bowl of cold water for five minutes, then lay out to dry.

HONEYCOMB
Honeycomb is the waxy secretions of worker bees to store their larvae, honey, and pollen. As the hexagonal cylinders of honeycomb are filled with honey, they are capped by bees with yet another layer

of wax. Honeycomb is a completely natural product that carries myriad health benefits, is fun to eat, and makes an impressive cocktail garnish.

MARSHMALLOWS

The gooey treat now called marshmallow was enjoyed by Egyptian royalty as early as 2000 BC. Americans today purchase 90 million pounds of marshmallows each year, equivalent to the weight of 1,286 gray whales. Ligonier, Indiana is the self described marshmallow capital of the world and hosts the annual Toasted Marshmallow Day on August 30.

NUTMEG

Native to the Spice Islands of the South Pacific, nutmeg is treasured for its fresh, rich aroma and woody, bittersweet flavor with hints of clove. Nutmeg can be easily ground using the fine side of a cheese grater and sprinkled onto warm drinks and cocktails.

THE RIMS

Why do we rim our cocktails?
Presentation, of course, is important, but a thoughtfully rimmed cocktail provides texture, color, and contrasting flavors to drinks like Margaritas or Bloody Marys.

EVERY RIM IS COMPRISED OF
TWO COMPONENTS:

LIQUID	SOLID
simple syrup	salt
lime juice	sugar
melted chocolate	crushed candies
rim glue	spices
	herbs

TIPS FOR flawless COCKTAIL RIMS

Choose your ingredients wisely. Everything that touches the rim of a glass will affect the flavor of the drink.

Pour some of your preferred rimming liquid into a shallow dish. Roll the outer circumference of the glass in the liquid. Put your chosen solid in a similarly shallow dish and repeat the process with the moistened segment of your glass.

For more precise, easy and fun rimming experience check out our new mixology line by Cocktail Vision, distributed by ChefRubber.com

SALT

As cocktail makers and drinkers have become sophisticated, salt has found a regular home behind the bar. Salt can awaken the most dormant ingredient, balance a cocktail's acidity and enhance the complexity of a cocktail with exciting new layers. Infused salts can be used to rim a cocktail glass for added color and flavor. Saline solution, made by dissolving salt in boiling water, can be sparingly added to cocktails from an eye dropper or dasher bottle.

ChefRubber, SaltWorks, Salt Traders feature an extensive collection of gourmet salts.

STAR ANISE

Star anise is the eight-pointed, star-shaped seed pod from the fruit of an evergreen shrub native to China. Both the seeds and pod, whole or ground, are used to impart an exotic, sweet anise flavor to food and cocktail recipes.

STRAWBERRIES

Packed with nutrients, organic strawberries impart health benefits along with lively acidity, bright berry flavors and floral juiciness to your cocktails. Make sure to only consume organically-grown berries for optimal flavor and health benefits.

VANILLA

One of the most labor-intensive and expensive crops, vanilla is the hand-pollinated and harvested fruit of an orchid that blossoms for only a few hours each year. After curing for several months, the vanilla bean shrivels to one-quarter of its original size, losing 80 percent of its moisture content, and developing its rich and fragrant aroma. Though you can purchase vanilla as a bean, mashed paste, powder, or liquid extract, whole beans have a more complex vanilla flavor than extract and make for a beautifully-exotic cocktail garnish.

COCKTAIL SHAKER VS MIXING GLASS

Mixing a cocktail with ice not only combines and chills the ingredients, it also creates a desired dilution which allows tertiary flavors to form in the cocktail. Stirring in a mixing glass is a gentle method of incorporating and chilling the cocktail without modification of its texture, used for spirit-forward cocktails such as an Old Fashioned or a Negroni. Shaking, on the other hand, introduces aeration and icy texture to your beverage, used for less alcoholic and refreshing cocktails. Regardless of the mixing method, it is crucial to strain out the old ice and serve the cocktail either "up" or over fresh ice, ensuring the cocktail is consumed as intended without being watered down.

DOUBLE STRAINING

Double straining is a process of straining the cocktail liquid through a Hawthorne strainer followed by a mesh strainer on its way to the glass. This allows removal of finer shards of ice and any remaining particles such as pulp or seeds, resulting in a perfectly clean, silky cocktail.

HAWTHORN STRAINER

A hawthorn strainer has a flat top with a semi-circle coil underneath, designed to fit snugly inside a shaker tin to hold back ice and solid ingredients, creating a clean, crisp cocktail in the glass. To use a hawthorn strainer, place it inside the mixing tin, coil facing down. While holding the strainer in place with your forefinger and mixing tin with the rest of your hand, slowly tip the tin over the serving glass.

JULEP STRAINER

When straining a cocktail from a mixing glass, place a julep strainer inside the mixing glass with the bowl of the spoon facing out. Hold the strainer on the joint between the handle and bowl using your forefinger, firmly grasp the glass close to the rim, and slowly tip the mixing glass over the serving glass.

THE GLASSWARE

In recent years, the renewed interest in classic cocktails is due to our fascination with the elegant and whimsical glassware that they are served in. I am one of many who believe that glassware does make a difference. Your cocktail experience starts at first sight and first touch. Your serving vessel is your artistic canvas and taking particular care with presentation will elevate the entire experience. Here are a few essentials to consider for you mixology collection:

STEMWARE

Category of glassware of various shapes and sizes with a glass "stem" as a trait in common. Cocktails presented in stemware are usually served 'up'. I recommend chilling stemware in the freezer before using it, to help maintain the cocktail's ideal temperature. Cocktail Coupe, Nick & Nora glass, martini glass, champagne flute are some of the examples.

ROCKS GLASS

Also known as Old Fashioned Glass or a tumbler. It's a low glass with straight sides and heavy bottom. It is durable and large enough to accommodate an ice rock. Cocktails served in a rocks glass are usually spirit-forward and meant to be consumed slowly, however, despite the name, they don't necessarily need to include ice and can be served "neat".

HIGHBALL OR COLLINS GLASS

Usually a tall, narrow glass designed to serve fizzy cocktails on ice. This shape of a glass is ideal for cocktails that include carbonated mixers like soda water or ginger beer. Carbonation dissipates easily from liquid at the surface which is minimized in a slender glassware.

THE BIOGRAPHY

"Just look pretty, sell as many frozen drinks as possible, and sell an extra shot or two of booze," my boss instructed me. This where my mixology journey began, like all great things, in sleazy obscurity. At the age of twenty one, I was hired as a bartender for a daiquiri bar on The Las Vegas Strip. Originally from a small village in Russia, I had no clue what comprised a Rum and Coke or Gin and Tonic, except perhaps the Coke. I was strong even in high heels, carrying as many drinks as would fit onto two trays at once. It fascinated me how different a blue, red or yellow slushy tasted, depending on what spirit was added to it. I was instantly hooked on the entire scene.

My twenties flew by with increasing sophistication and decreasing crushed ice, at the same time "high-end" cocktails became mainstream. I found myself and the industry evolving away from those simple, sweet ole' days selling yard-long slushees taking nothing away from that quintessential Vegas experience. I also found myself closer to my Russian roots of resourcefulness and stylistic restraint. With extremely limited options for ingredients, I was accustomed to improvisation and creativity ever since I was a child. Artisanal mixology is, after all, best achieved combining well-chosen ingredients sparingly in a shaker instead of dumped into a blender.

Whether recreating a beloved classic or fashioning a novel libation, I approach the craft of mixology as a chef would create an entree. An intimate knowledge of ingredients and their synergy is key. Traveling the world, I've been blessed to have experienced a wealth of cultures, their unique cuisines and their rainbow of distillates. Classically trained in art, I understand the essence of good orchestration — a perspective I use to build and integrate the flavor components of a cocktail. My special power, were I a superhero, is my mental library of flavors I've cataloged over the years. My second superpower is my ability to imagine the interaction of those thousands of flavor combinations in my head. It saves money on booze, trust me.

I find my purpose leading people through a well-provisioned cocktail journey, as does a seasoned expedition guide through the jungle. The spirit safari, if you will, begins upon opening the menu — better yet, the spirit story book. What enchanted libation will you be experiencing tonight? "Peachcraft" or "Voodoo Brew"? Each masterpiece is custom built, uniquely garnished and lovingly poured to evoke the senses and help carry you away on an unforgettable cocktail adventure. I achieve my inner zen in the joy shown on the faces of others while sipping my creations and enjoying the journey I've thoughtfully curated for them.

Let Cocktail Vision be your spirit guide!